Neigóon
NAGOONBERRY

Kanat'á
BLUEBERRY

A NOTE TO THE Forager:
Please only gather berries & other
wild foods that you & an experienced
adult can identify beyond a doubt.
There are many toxic look-alikes.
Gunalchéesh!

Tínx
CROWBERRY

Lingít shákw
STRAWBERRY

For ax̱ léelk'w and Grammy

About This Book

The illustrations for this book were done in watercolor and mixed media. This book was edited by Susan Rich and designed by Saho Fujii and Lynn El-Roeiy. The production was supervised by Nyamekye Waliyaya, and the production editor was Jen Graham. The text was set in Ashbury, and the display type is hand-lettered.

BERRY Song

Michaela Goade

L B

LITTLE, BROWN AND COMPANY

New York   Boston

On an island at the edge of a wide, wild sea,
Grandma shows me how to live on the land.

Together we pull
hemlock branches
from the salty ocean,
heavy with herring eggs
like tiny stars.

On the beach, we
gather ribbons of
slippery seaweed
dancing in the tide.

By the tumbling, icy falls,
we dip our nets for
silvery salmon hidden
beneath the current.

And in the forest…

we pick berries.

Salmonberry, Cloudberry, Blueberry, Nagoonberry.
Huckleberry, Soapberry, Strawberry, Crowberry.

The berries sing to us, glowing like little jewels.
We sing too, so berry—and bear—know we are here.

Grandma tells me,
"We speak
to the land…"

"As the land
speaks to us,"
I say.

Huckleberry, Soapberry, Strawberry, Crowberry.
Thimbleberry, Swampberry, Bogberry, Chalkberry.

The forest sings to us,
through misting rain
and whoosh of wing,
the sweet smell of cedar
and the tickle of moss.

We sing too, so the land knows we are grateful.

Grandma tells me,
"We take care
of the land…"

"As the land takes care of us.
Gunalchéesh," I say,
giving thanks.

Thimbleberry, Swampberry, Bogberry, Chalkberry.
Lingonberry, Raspberry, Bunchberry, Cranberry.

Our ancestors sing to us,
their voices dancing
on wind and water.
We sing too, so they know
that we'll always remember.

And we sing for the future,
so that all will hear
and all will know
this beautiful berry song.

Grandma tells me,
"We are a part
of the land…"

"As the land
   is a part of us,"
   I say.

The ocean sings to us,
rolling ashore
like a beating drum.

We sing too, so the tides know we are home.

Together we make salmonberry syrup and cranberry marmalade until the kitchen glows like a summer sky.

We feast on huckleberry pie
and strawberry crisp,
raspberry scones and
freshly whipped soapberries.

We share gifts of blueberry
jelly and nagoonberry jam.

"Gunalchéesh," we say,
giving thanks.

The nights grow long, edged in frost,
as sea fades gently into sky.
The forest is resting,
the forest is dreaming,
waiting for berry song.

And so the seasons change.

On an island at the edge
of a wide, wild sea,
I take my little sister's hand.

Lingonberry, Raspberry,
Bunchberry, Cranberry.
Salmonberry, Cloudberry,
Blueberry, Nagoonberry.

"I have so much to show you."

A Note from the Author

 In the land of tléikw...

Like the young girl in this book, I too live on an island at the edge of a wide, wild sea where I grew up picking tléikw, or berries. My home is Sheet'ká, or Sitka, Alaska. It is the same island my Tlingit grandmother, great-grandparents, and great-great-grandparents called home. All year long I excitedly wait for berry season, for the juicy salmonberries that strum the first notes of berry song, and the cranberries after the first freeze that signal its end. Every time I wander back into the forest, I am a little kid again, spellbound by the magic and joy of berry song.

As Tlingit people, our way of life has always been woven into the rhythm of the land and sea, to the animals and plants that nurture our body and spirit. It has always meant more than food or survival. This way of life honors a deep kinship with the land rooted in respect, balance, and reciprocity. Tlingit values teach us to treat the land and our nonhuman kin with great reverence and gratitude, and it is often during traditional food-harvesting practices such as berry picking when ancestral knowledge and values are passed down from one generation to the next.

Berries have always been a celebrated part of Tlingit life. They are a traditional diet staple providing essential nutrients, eaten fresh or preserved with fish or seal oil, or pressed and dried into berry cakes. Today we also process berries through freezing, canning, or baking delicious treats! Historically, berries were used as medicine, trade goods, ceremonial gifts, and symbols of wealth and prestige; and much like hunting grounds or salmon streams, certain berry patches were claimed and stewarded by different clans. Traditional stories tell us of the importance of berries—how they nourished a young boy climbing his chain of arrows to the moon, or how Raven taught us to preserve them. Berries are one of the most important foods brought out during a koo.éex', a major ceremonial and often memorial gathering. Berries hold great symbolic and spiritual significance. They connect us to land, community, and culture. They remind us of home.

When I am out picking berries, I feel rooted in the land. If I am sad or troubled before entering the forest, I always leave happy. Berry picking is medicine. Berries are gifts from the earth, gathered and shared in gratitude. When I am lost in a patch of salmonberries that drip from the leaves in hues of sunshine, coral, and ruby, I am in awe of Mother Earth's many gifts, and I try my best to listen—to the berries, to the forest and water, to Raven's musical call, to my Tlingit ancestors and the children yet to come. I hear the same sparkling song in my grandmother's chuckle as she tells me about summers at the salmon cannery with her family, when coming home with a bucket full of berries spared her from any scolding. I hear the same chorus in my mother's voice as she passes along the wisdom of my great-aunt: "When the blueberry leaves start to turn red, that's when the fruit is sweetest." And I hear that same melody in my young nephew, when together we sing and sway through a mountainside meadow, our hearts—much like our buckets and baskets—full to the brim. "Gunalchéesh," I teach him to say, giving thanks. The song is everywhere, if you listen. Can you hear it?

Was'x'aan tléigu   Dáxw or K'eishkaháagu   Kanat'á   Tleikatánk

Listening offers a powerful opportunity to build a deeper kinship with the land. Among its many lessons are the ones shared in this book:

 We speak to the land as the land speaks to us.

The land is alive. Everything has spirit. Talk to the berries. Learn their Indigenous names. Ask them for permission to be harvested. Thank them. There is a magnificent symphony of song that goes into making one small berry—the sun, rain, and wind do their part. So do the salmon, birds, and bears, whose life cycles and foraging fertilize the forest and spread berry seeds. Other animals help spread the seeds too, including humans! The hummingbirds, bees, butterflies, and other insects help when they pollinate the berry blossoms, as do the ancient trees that die and nourish the soil. When you speak to the land and listen in return, you'll be amazed at what you learn.

 We take care of the land as the land takes care of us.

As the land gives to us, it is our responsibility to give in return. When picking berries, it is important to be respectful. We share the forest. Take only what you need and can sensibly process, leaving berries behind for our animal relatives. Taking care of the land also means protecting Mother Earth in a larger sense. Learning about commercial fishery overharvesting, oil pipelines, mining, logging, and other damaging and unsustainable human industries is a great place to start. Protesting, contacting legislators, voting, volunteering with local environmental groups, thinking about where you spend your money, and sharing what you learn are just a few ways to get involved. Together we can unite in defense of Mother Earth, becoming caretakers and ensuring a future for all.

 We are a part of the land as the land is a part of us.

We are not separate from the natural world. Even in the city, nature is all around us. It is all one song. The Tongass National Forest, where my family and I live, and where I set this story, is the largest intact temperate rain forest in the world and the largest national forest in the United States. Not only is it incredibly important to us humans and our nonhuman relatives that live here, but it is vital in helping combat the global climate crisis. The Tongass is home to the traditional territories of the Tlingit, Haida, and Tsimshian nations, who have coexisted in balance with the land since time immemorial. Today, Native and non-Native people work together to protect these wild lands. Indigenous history and rights, land sovereignty, and environmental justice are closely intertwined, and I encourage you to listen to and lift Indigenous voices. In many places around the world, Indigenous peoples are leading the way in protecting our planet. I encourage you to find out whose traditional territory you call home, learn about their history and the issues they are facing today, and seek ways to engage.

Gunalchéesh!

Neigóon   Lingít shákw

Ch'ee<u>x</u>'
THIMBLEBERRY

Kaneilts'ákw
SWAMPBERRY/
BLACK CURRANT

Dáxw
OR <u>K</u>'eishkaháagu
LINGONBERRY

Tlé<u>k</u>w yádi
RASPBERRY